Tam Gu
Quest of the Four Friends

Tam Gu
Quest of the Four Friends

by James Theros

Printed in the United States of America.

For information address Level 10 Publishing at
33863 US Highway 19 N., Palm Harbor, FL 34684

Copies of this book may be purchased for educational,
business, or sales promotional use.
For information please write or email:

Level 10 Publishing
33863 US Highway 19 N.
Palm Harbor, FL 34684

MasterTheros@yahoo.com

FIRST EDITION
ISBN-13: 978-0-9904164-1-8

Library of Congress Cataloging-in-Publication Data
Tam Gu: Quest of the Four Friends, first edition,
James Theros

Interior book design by Sue Balcer, JustYourType.biz

Chapter
One

It was a beautiful, warm summer day. Four friends were about to meet up at the neighborhood park for some early-morning fun and games.

The local park was their favorite place to meet during the summer. Sally was usually the first to arrive, worn-out leather mitt in hand. She was the fussiest of the four friends. She always wanted to make sure that there were no rocks or sticks on the ground near where they played baseball.

The other neighborhood kids generally showed up at the last minute. It didn't matter, though, because Sally made sure that they got the very best spot on the field.

Joey always seemed to be the second one to arrive.

He always brought two bats with him. His favorite was his trusty Louisville Slugger, given to him by one of the local teams, and reportedly used by the Great Bambino, himself, to knock 'em out of the park!

Of course, there is no way to know for sure if the bat was actually used by Babe Ruth, but Joey didn't seem to care. He knew in his heart that this bat was the real deal, and he made sure to clean it and wax it after every game.

Joey also brought along a shiny blue aluminum bat. The bat had a big dent near the top, most likely from using it to practice swinging at fast balls thrown by his friend, Billy.

He practiced throwing baseballs almost as much as most people practice walking. There was even a rumor going around that Billy slept with his baseball, took baths with it, and even had a secret name for it! *The Bullet.*

For a young man of only 11 years old, Billy threw the ball as fast as any high school-aged pitcher in the area.

Billy was usually the last to arrive, and it was often a few minutes after Sam. Sam was the team's fastest runner, and he made sure everyone knew how fast he was. He made a race out of everything, including racing his sister, Sally, to school each morning.

The two would start on the front porch and explode like race cars from the last step of the porch. They both continued in a full sprint, until one of them, usually Sam, tagged the flag pole out in front of their school. The flag pole was their official finish line. It also became the new starting line for the inevitable race home right after school let out each day.

When the school bell rang in the afternoon, Sam was the first kid to have his backpack in order. He also made sure his shoe laces were always tied extra tight, to give him more support so he could run faster.

Sally knew it was important for Sam to win these races, so she usually allowed him to win. She always pretended to get tired about half way through each race. She would smile as her younger brother passed her and extended his index finger in victory.

She never let on that she could beat Sam with ease, and she did her best to make sure she always looked out for him.

As the four friends arrived at the park, they began talking about their game that was to begin shortly.

Joey strolled up, bats in hand, mouth full of enough chewing gum to choke a small horse. After blowing what had to have been one of the biggest bubble gum bubbles in the history of bubble gum bubbles, it popped and stuck to Joey's chin.

Joey started peeling it off, wiped his hand on his pants, and put the gum right back into his mouth. He immediately began creating another huge, pink bubble. He was careful this time, not to blow such a big bubble. As it popped, he sucked it back into his mouth and said to Billy, "Hey, do you see that bush over there? Why don't you go and grab some of the leaves and we'll use them to mark the bases for today's game."

Billy nodded and skipped over to the bush, when something shiny caught his eye from underneath.

He bent down to see what it was, reached inside the bush with a stick, and touched it. As soon as he touched it, the object began glowing with a pulsing white light that made him have to squint to see it.

With a clever little pulling action, Billy used the stick to move the object closer towards him. He then reached out and grabbed it.

"Hey guys! Look what I found!" he yelled.

Sally, Joey and Sam all rushed over to see what the object was.

"Woah," said Sam. "I've never seen anything like it before!"

"Me, either," said Sally. The object was now reflecting in her eyes and lighting her face up with its strange, glowing light.

Joey reached out and grabbed the object, and it began to glow less intensely now. It became clear to the kids what the object was. A small, beautiful, silver box with what looked like ancient Chinese inscriptions on it. There was a large Chinese character on the center of the top of the box.

"What do you think is inside?" asked Joey.

"I don't know," said Sally, "but let's open it and find out."

Joey began to open the box, but as he did the box started glowing again. The harder he pulled on the top of the box, the more intense the glow became.

"This is incredible!" said Joey to the group.

"I can't seem to open it."

Sam looked at Billy, and Billy looked at Sally. All three looked back at Joey, as he handed the small silver box to Sally.

"Here, maybe you can open it."

Sally cautiously took the box from Joey. Just as her dirt-caked fingers touched the box, it began to make a low-pitched humming sound. Then, it slowly began opening on its own.

"How did you do that?!" remarked Joey, his face in complete disbelief.

"I.... I don't know," said Sally. "I just took it from you and it's opening all by itself."

The box continued to open and the glow on the outside completely stopped.

Inside the box was a plush, red felt pad, and right in the center was what appeared to be a scroll of some sort.

Sally carefully removed the scroll. As she began slowly unrolling it, being careful not to damage it, a flash of light lit the sky around them. In an instant, the four friends were transported through space and time. They suddenly found themselves in what appeared to be a large forest. There were hundreds and hundreds of incredibly tall trees. Much taller than they had ever seen before.....anywhere on the planet!

Chapter
Two

Strange animals lined the trees; animals that nobody had ever seen before. There were all types of insects that had never been seen before, either. The sounds that they emitted were peaceful, heavenly, and, strangely-enough, quite calming.

The sounds of a babbling brook could be heard in the distance. A warm, gentle wind brought the lovely scent of some of the incredibly beautiful flowers and greenery to their noses.

Joey, Billy, Sally and Sam stood in complete disbelief. They took turns looking into each other's eyes, searching for answers.

What had just happened to them?

The four stood in the same spot for what seemed like forever. Each refusing to believe that this was not a dream, and hoping that someone would wake them from it soon!

About a hundred yards away, they heard a faint humming sound.

They cautiously approached the area where the sound was coming from.

As they got closer, the sound grew louder. Through the trees and plants, they could see a tall, shadowy figure moving very slowly. He seemed to be moving in some type of pre-arranged pattern.

The humming noise was coming from the feet of the shadowy figure.

Billy began moving towards it. Sally
quickly rolled up the scroll and put it into
her pocket, as she grabbed Billy by the
sleeve. She pulled him back and quietly
scolded him.

"What in the world do you think you're
doing?!" Sally asked him.

"Don't you want to see what that is......
who that is?" replied Billy.

Joey chimed in and said, "Yeah, I wanna
see too!"

Sam, still in shock from all that had just
happened, silently stared at the other three.
He obviously didn't know what to say.

Sally spoke up, "OK. But let's be quiet and
take our time. After all, we don't even know
what that is, or if it is friendly.............. or
dangerous."

The boys nodded in agreement, as they
slowly started their approach.

Sally peeled back a few of the thick, tropical, green leaves as they moved closer and closer.

As they stepped out into the area where the shadowy figure was, they noticed that it was not a human.

The kids gasped in fear. Somehow, though, they felt a strange sense of kindness and safety that radiated from the creature.

Sam finally spoke up, "I can't believe what I'm seeing!" he exclaimed.

"He looks like a lion mixed with a tall human!"

The creature had the basic body of a tall middle-aged man. He had the head of a lion (complete with an orange mane).... and piercing blue eyes that looked like they could stare right into your soul.

The creature was wearing a long black robe with a strange symbol on the back of it. Sam thought the symbol looked like something he'd seen before but he couldn't exactly place it.

The creature continued moving about, the hum coming from his feet, as they seemed to be etching something into the ground beneath him.

As he was finishing his mysterious movements, Billy approached the creature from behind. Suddenly, the lion man leapt into the air, turned a full 180 degrees, and gently landed on the ground in front of Billy, without making the slightest sound.

His piercing blue eyes locked with Billy's, and softened, as a gentle smile came over his weathered face.

The creature seemed to be familiar with humans, almost as if he had seen them before.

He slowly lifted his long right arm as it protruded from the sleeve of his tattered black robe. He motioned the other three over to where he and Billy were standing.

The others cautiously approached. They now stood next to Billy so that all four of them were directly in front of the strange lion man. The kids formed a small semi-circle pattern in front of him.

The lion man pointed down to the ground beneath them. As they looked down, they noticed an elaborate Chinese symbol on the ground that he had created with the movements of his feet.

It was the very same symbol that was etched into the silver box they had found in the park!

"I am Saja Namja, but you may just call me Saja," he said, as the edges of his eyes began to widen a bit. "I have been entrusted as the guardian of this place for many, many years. I have been expecting you."

Sally nearly interrupted him when she said, "Eh...Expecting us?! How could you be *expecting* us?!"

Saja Namja calmly turned towards her and continued speaking. "Young lady, do you remember that little silver box you found?"

"I found it! I found the box!" exclaimed Billy. "I was the one who found it."

"Actually," continued Saja, "the box found *you*. You see, the box is over 5,000 years old, and has been found before by some of the world's most successful people. People you probably know quite well....... and many whom, I'm quite certain, you've never even heard of before.

You see, when the box finds the right person (or people, as in your case) it begins to glow. Once it is picked up it can only be opened by a true leader. So, if the person who is holding the box is not yet a true leader, he or she will not be able to open it. When the box is held by a leader with an honest heart, the box opens on its own and reveals it contents to that person."

Suddenly, Sally remembered the scroll and reached into her pocket to retrieve it. After struggling with her pocket for a moment, she removed it and held it up towards Saja.

"Ah yes, the Scroll of Mingyun," said Saja. "Have you had a chance to read it?"

"No. I have not. One minute we were standing in the park, getting ready to play a game of baseball, and the very next moment, we were here in this strange place," Sally said. She was now beginning to realize that this was not some silly dream, after all.

They were actually standing here, speaking to a man who had the head of a lion!

"Would you like to know what happened to you?" Saja asked.

Joey, Sam and Billy, in unison, replied, "Please! Tell us what happened!"

"We are not any place that any of us recognize," said Sam. "I just want to go home. Please. Can you help us find our way home?"

Saja took a deep breath and contemplated his next words very carefully. "When the box opened and Sally touched the scroll, she connected you with a parallel universe. You have been transported here for a very special quest. To return home, you must first complete the quest."

Chapter

Three

"Q-Q-Quest? What are you talking about, Saja? I never asked to be part of any quest," said Joey.

"Ah, that may be true, but sometimes the quest chooses *you*. As I said, the box chose you....... and it chose you for a very good reason.

This is not any ordinary quest, though." said Saja. "This quest is known in our world as the 'Tam Gu.' The Tam Gu is an ancient and sacred quest. It can only be completed by the most dedicated and sincere people from your universe.

It is said that whoever is able to complete the Tam Gu will be gifted with special powers and mental abilities. These abilities will make all life's endeavors more successful.

Let me ask you a question........Have you ever heard of George Washington or Abraham Lincoln?" asked Saja.

"Of course we have! They were some of our country's first presidents!" exclaimed Billy.

"Yes. And they, along with many others, completed the same quest that is now in front of you.

Maybe you've heard of Trisha Birnbaum?"

"Trisha Birnbaum?! She used to go to my school! She was the president of the student council for our school before I started going there. There were pictures of her everywhere. Lots of her trophies were in the glass cases in the hallways, too. She had skills in nearly every school sport there was!

She then went on to high school and graduated as the valedictorian of the entire school. She gave a speech at graduation that led to her being invited to become one of the newscasters on Channel 13! She's probably the most successful person to ever come out of our city," said Sally.

"She's been an incredible role model to me, even if I never got to meet her in person."

"Yes," said Saja, "That is correct. But, what you may find surprising is that she, too, completed the Tam Gu. Completing the Tam Gu allowed her to accomplish so many things in her life. It's also why she will accomplish many more things in the future."

"Wow," said Sally, slowly shaking her head in disbelief. "I had no idea."

"I don't care about quests," said Joey. "I just want to go home and play baseball!"

Billy spoke up and said, "I don't know......
it kind of sounds like fun to me.

What do you think, Sam?"

"If you're up for it, I'm up for it, Sam replied.

Billy then turned and asked, "How about you, Sally?"

Sally wasted no time in coming to a decision.

"If Trisha Birnbaum did it, I don't even have to know what it is. Whatever it is, if it will do even one-tenth of what it did for her, I'm in!"

Joey, with a look of guilt on his face, then spoke up, "Oh.....OK. If you guys are in, I guess you can count me in, too."

"Very good," said Saja. "But you must understand that, once you begin, you cannot quit until the quest is complete. If you do not complete the quest, you will not be able to return home."

The four friends immediately felt butterflies in their stomachs upon hearing those words.

"The Tam Gu has 4 separate challenges. Some of them are mental, while others are physical. Each of you has your own unique gifting, which will play a part in the success of your quest. To succeed, you must use these items," said Saja. He reached into his robe and removed another silver box, exactly like the one the kids had found in the park.

"Inside this box are 3 more small scrolls. They contain the secrets you will need to be able to handle each of the 4 challenges of the Tam Gu."

Saja then handed the box to Sally, and as she accepted it, the box glowed and then opened on its own. Inside were the three smaller scrolls.

The first one read,

The second small scroll read:

The Five
Tenets:
Courtesy,
Integrity,
Perseverance,
Self-Control,
Indomitable Spirit

You must remember these in
moments of chaos or uncertainty

The third small scroll said:

> To Master Physical
> Skills Use These
> Six Ingredients:
> The 3 C's
> (Clean, Crisp,
> Clear) And
> The S.P.I. Principle
> (Speed, Power, Intensity)

"One more thing," said Saja. "The Scroll of Mingyun has magical qualities to it. Only one task will appear on the scroll at a time. To see what the next task is, you must first complete the task listed on the scroll. Once the task is complete, the next task will then reveal itself."

"Can you at least tell us what the 4 tasks are?" asked Billy, who usually spoke before thinking too much.

Saja turned to Billy, and replied, "There are 4 other important keys to completing this quest. You must promise me that you will remember what I am about to tell you and put them to use at the right moments."

With another impatient outburst, Billy said, "How will I know when the right moments are?"

"You'll know. When the time is right, you will just know," Saja replied.

"Billy lowered his head, nodded, and said, "I will, Saja. I promise."

Taking another deep breath, Saja raised his arms above his head. A strong wind came out of nowhere. Using only his index claw, he wrote the words *Patience, Respect, Modesty* and *Honesty* in the air. The brilliant, glowing gold letters gently floated in front of Billy. The light from the letters lit up his face before slowly fading away.

"These are the 4 cornerstones of mental training. They most-often come into play when we least want them to," Saja said. "The first one.... Patience..... is the will-ingness to wait. It is not necessary to know everything before beginning...... or even after beginning it."

A strange look came over Billy, as the words that he had read, written in the air in front of him, began to make sense.

"I understand, Saja. I can see how having patience might work to my benefit on this quest." Billy continued, "I never thought of it quite that way before. I will work towards improving my thoughts and behaviors so that I can complete this quest and bring honor to you. Thank you for sharing your wisdom with me, Saja."

Saja then turned and went back to his strange movements, as the humming sound from his feet began again. He began etching another symbol on the ground near the kids.

"Open the scroll, Sally," Saja said over his back, "and read the first task to your friends. Your quest begins this instant."

Sally relaxed the tight grip she had on the Scroll of Mingyun. She carefully opened it, and as she did, the first task slowly appeared on the weathered, papyrus paper. The ink glowed a beautiful gold. The letters first appeared in Chinese, and slowly transformed into letters that Sally recognized.

At the very top of the scroll, the words, "Scroll of Mingyun" appeared. About an inch underneath, the first task appeared...

Scroll of Mingyun Task One

To complete this task, you must first master the 3 basic stances (The horse stance, the front stance and the back stance).

When you are able to hold each one with perfect form for sixty seconds, without rising up between stances, you will have completed the first task.

Then, Saja stopped his motions again, and said to the four, "Go now, to the edge of this forest. There, you will find a flowing stream with a large boulder blocking the water's path. You will find an open area with a similar symbol etched into the ground. Stay there and practice the basic stances until you are successful with the task. When the first task is complete, you will hear a soft bell ring from the first silver box. A green checkmark will then appear on the left side of the task.

When you hear the bell, sit down by the water and discuss what you learned with each other.

You will then hear a second bell. That is your cue to open the scroll again to see the next task.

I will be observing you from a distance and will always be close by. Should you need anything, call out my name, and I will appear to you.

Before you leave, I will teach you the 3 stances. You must pay very close attention, though. If you do not perform them properly, you will not be able to complete the first task."

Sally, Sam, Billy and Joey moved towards Saja, as he instructed them on the important points of each of the 3 stances.

"The first stance is the horse stance. For this stance, the knees must bend to the point that your knees end up positioned over the feet. Push the knees out to the sides. The back must be kept straight, as if leaning against a tree. The fists should be held at the rib cage, with the elbows pulled back. Keep your toes pointing straight forward also, or you will lack balance and stability.

The second stance is the front stance. For this stance, bend your front knee enough that a person could sit on your bent leg without sliding off. The back leg must be kept completely straight. You should be able to support somebody's weight if they were to jump up onto the back of your straight leg. The toes of the front foot should be pointing forward, and ever so slightly inward. The toes of your back foot should also be facing towards the front. You will need strong legs to complete this task, and each of the other tasks of the Tam Gu. There should be approximately a space of about the width of your shoulders between your two feet. Your shoulders should be squarely facing the front.

The final stance is the back stance. For this stance, make sure your heels are on the same line. Your front foot points straight forward, while your back foot points out to the side.

You will want to bend your knees sharply, so that approximately 60 percent of your weight is on your back leg. The hands can be kept in fists on the ribs, same as the other stances."

With those instructions, Saja sat down over the Chinese character he had etched into the ground. He pulled the hood of his black robe up over his head, and went into a deep meditative state.

The four friends gave one last look at each other. Then, Sally began walking towards the edge of the forest, as Saja had instructed. The others followed, and the four friends set out to begin their first task.

Chapter

Four

As the kids approached the babbling brook Saja had told them about, they saw the huge boulder blocking the water. It created a beautiful cascading sound. Then, they noticed a clearing up ahead. As the kids inched closer, they could hear the soothing sounds of the brook, and it calmed their spirits... if only for a brief moment.

They stepped out of the forest and into the clearing, where Saja had instructed them to go. There, they found the Chinese character etched into the ground; by Saja, no doubt.

Sally gathered her strength as she tried to keep her fears hidden. She spoke up and said, "Alright, you heard what Saja said. We must master the 3 basic stances. Sam, you stand over here, Billy, you over here, and Joey, you over there."

The boys, mesmerized by their surroundings, and still wondering how Saja managed to create these beautiful designs on the ground with his feet, snapped out of their dazes, and moved into the positions that Sally had given each of them.

Sally stood in front of the boys and began to practice the first stance. It seemed simple at first. Then she realized that it probably couldn't be quite this easy. She thought back to the instructions that Saja had given them about the horse stance.

She looked down and noticed that her feet were pointing outward, and that she was only bending her knees a little. Then, she looked at the boys. She noticed that Billy was bending forward and resting his arms on his legs, which seemed to make it easier. Joey had his feet too close together and was squatting way too low for the stance to be correct. She thought to herself, "Hmmm, Joey's stance looks a little weird."

Then, she looked over at her brother, Sam. She noticed that Sam had a pained look on his face, and his legs were shaking uncontrollably.

"Sam, what's the matter? Are you OK?"

"I-I'm making sure that I'm doing everything that Saja told me to do, and it hurts. It hurts."

Joey took notice. He realized that he wasn't putting enough effort into his own stance. He looked at Sam, spread his feet a little wider, and came up just a little bit. He made sure that it looked like he was sitting on a bench, his knees now pushed out over his feet.

Billy also took note and straightened his back. Sally turned her toes straight ahead and sank lower into her stance.

Suddenly, the others' stances began looking more like Sam's. The other three kids then began experiencing the same things Sam was experiencing. Their legs began to tremble, too, as their muscles grew tired.

They each lasted about 23 seconds. Then they all stood up and leaned over to rest on their straightened legs. Sweat was now glistening in the moon light from their foreheads and necks.

"Wow. This is a *lot* harder than I thought it was going to be," said Sally. "Saja made it look so easy."

The kids took a quick break and then tried again.

Each time they tried, they were able to add several seconds to their time. When they got up to about 37 seconds, Sally said to the others, "OK, now, let's try the next stance."

The next stance proved to be the tiniest bit simpler than the horse stance. The front stance allowed them to rest their back legs a little, because most of the weight was on the front leg.

They had a bit less trouble getting the front stance to look and feel right. They were easily able to hold this stance for 30 seconds before their legs grew tired again.

Joey suggested that they go down to the brook and get some water.

The others agreed, and they started walking towards the water. They laid down on their stomachs, near the edge of the water, and cupped their hands together to scoop up as much as possible before it fell to the ground.

The water seemed to have a pleasant quality to it. It tasted so pure and clean. The water cooled their throats as it dribbled down the sides of their cheeks and onto their shirts.

"This water is SO good!" exclaimed Sam. "I used to drink milk or soda when I was thirsty. I feel like this water is healing my body. When I get back home, I'm going to start drinking more water and less of the other things I used to drink."

Hearing this pleased Saja, who was close by, watching and listening to the four friends as they tackled their very first task.

After drinking enough water, they sat over the Chinese character on the ground and spent a few minutes thinking about the last of the 3 basic stances.

Then, Sally looked at the boys and said, "OK, we don't have much time to lose. We have to master the third stance."

The back stance was going to be the most challenging of the three stances. Not only did they have to bend both knees sharply, but they also had to pay attention to the different positions of each foot.

As they stood up and got into the stance, they realized that it was very much like the horse stance. Billy remembered Saja telling him that he had to point the toes of his front foot forward, while leaving the toes of his back foot pointed to the side.

Billy made sure everyone was doing this, and the group was able to stay in the stance for a very long time. They made it a full 58 seconds before their legs gave out again!

They went back to the brook once again and each of the friends drank more of the magical water.

After heading back to the clearing, Sally told the boys, "OK Guys, we've proven that we can do these stances. It took us a little while to get them down, but if we use our focus and discipline, I'm sure we can hold each one for 60 seconds."

"Yes," said Billy. "I know we can do it. If we each do our very best and work as a team, we can do most anything!"

The others looked at Billy with pride in their eyes. They exchanged glances, nodded at Sally, and got mentally ready to give it a shot.

"Alright now, I will fight with every ounce of my being to stay in perfect form in all 3 of these stances. I just know that we can do this," Sally told the others.

They each moved into their positions and began the task. Once their horse stances were perfect, Sally began counting. "One, one-thousand, two, one-thousand, three, one-thousand, four........."

The magical water from the brook gave the kids the extra strength they needed. They held perfect horse stances, and smiled at each other when they realized they were going to be able to easily make it to 60 seconds.

"Front stance," said Sally. Everyone picked up their left foot and moved it slightly to the left. They each shifted their back foot to face the same direction, as well. Almost in perfect unison, they locked out their knees, and held picture-perfect front stances.

When the 60 seconds were about over, Joey noticed that Billy was beginning to show signs of fatigue. Billy was about to pop up to relieve the pain in his legs, but he looked back at Joey. Seeing Joey's determination inspired Billy to dig deep and fight through the pain. Billy then stayed in perfect form for the entire 60 seconds with the others.

As Sally finished counting the last number, Sam shouted, "Last stance guys! C'mon! We can make it!!"

Without getting up even an inch, they all pivoted their back feet so that they turned sideways. Then, they shifted their weight onto their back legs and into perfect back stances. They did this by drawing their front feet in so that the heels of both feet moved onto the very same line.

As the time ticked, they had to dig deep to keep from giving in to the pain they felt in their legs.

This time, Sally's face grew very red. It became obvious that she was fighting back tears. Sally continued counting... her voice beginning to quiver more with each number.

Her brother Sam noticed and told her, "Sally, you're the strongest person I know. Yes, it hurts. I hurt, too. But I know you can do this. Come on. We're almost there!"

After hearing the encouraging words from her little brother (and realizing that they were all feeling the same pain) Sally's voice sounded confident again.

"Fifty one, one-thousand, fifty two, one-thousand, fifty three, one-thousand, fifty four, one thousand....."

It seemed like an eternity.

When they heard the words, "Sixty, one-thousand" they heard the faint sound of a bell ring from someplace.

"Did you hear that?" asked Joey.

"Yes. I heard it, too." said Sally. "It was a bell."

"That's right! That's right!" said Billy. "That means we're supposed to sit down by the water and discuss what we learned from the task."

"Ok. Hurry. Let's go get another drink and then sit down and talk about what just happened," said Sam.

The four friends did as instructed and spent several minutes discussing all that they had learned from the first task.

The kids came to the realization that the biggest lesson they learned was that, if they focused on doing the stances properly, it made their legs hurt. The pain they felt made them want to give up.

But, together, they were stronger than any one person on the team. They realized that, if they worked together, and encouraged each other, they could do it. They also realized that they now had stronger legs from holding the stances. They felt like they could run faster, jump higher....... and who knows, what else.

As they high-fived each other and sat by the babbling brook, enjoying feeling the pride of accomplishment, they heard a second bell ring.

The first task was complete.

Sally, anxiously reached into her pocket and pulled out the scroll. She unraveled it, and, as Saja had told them, a green checkmark appeared next to the first task. Then the letters slowly transformed back into Chinese.

The second task then appeared. As the Chinese characters appeared on the scroll, they began to glow a bright, beautiful gold color, and changed into English, so the kids could read it.

Chapter

Five

As the glowing, Chinese characters began changing into English, the second task appeared:

Scroll of Mingyun
Task Two

To complete this task, you must first master the 3 basic kicks. The front snap kick, the roundhouse kick and the side kick.

When you are able to kick at head level and hold each kick for 2 seconds before setting your leg down, you will have completed the second task.

None of the four friends had ever thrown a kick, outside of playing kickball down at the park.

Ah, the park. It seemed like millions of miles away..... and that's because it *was* millions of miles away.

Just then, they got startled by the sound of a lion's roar off in the distance. They thought it might be Saja, but weren't sure. They only heard one roar and then silence. They waited for a few moments, but all they could hear was the peaceful sound of the strange insects around them.

Sally then spoke up, "OK guys, I'm sure Saja will be alright. The roar didn't sound like he was in trouble. In fact, it kind of reminded me of my dad's yawn in the morning."

Then, the expression on Sally's face changed.

"Aww, dad. I really miss him right now. I miss mom, too. Guys, we've got to get through this task so we can get home and see our parents again."

The others nodded in silence.

"How are we supposed to learn these kicks?" asked Joey.

"I don't know", said Sam. "I sure don't know how to do them."

A strange hum came from just up ahead, so, the kids followed the sound. As they got closer, they recognized it as the sound made by Saja's feet when he practiced his movements.

Billy ran ahead of the group and shouted, "Saja! Saja! I knew it was you!

But, we heard a lion's roar in the other direction a moment ago. We thought *that* was you!"

Saja's movements came to a slow halt, as he finished etching another Chinese character on the ground.

"I knew you'd be along any moment, so I have been preparing your second lesson. The sound that you heard was not from me, but from another creature that inhabits this land.

His voice may be like mine, but his heart is not. He used to be one of my students, but he stopped training with me and began using what I taught him for evil purposes. His name is Napun Saram.

At one time, he was my top pupil. When he stopped training with me, he started to teach fighting techniques to creatures who shouldn't have been taught. These creatures come from the other side of the forest, which is a very dangerous place to be.

Now, they roam this land, as bandits; attacking and robbing anyone they find.

If you see Napun or any of his followers, leave right away and do not look back. I will do my best to protect you from them. Each of these Etchings of Protection has some of my essence in them.

Napun Saram and the creatures that serve him cannot come near them. The etchings are like poison to his minions and him.

These characters are noble words. This one that I just finished says, 'Humility.'

To have humility is a noble characteristic and, so, it is repulsive to Napun and his followers. You will be safe as long as you are near one of my etchings."

"W-w-w-wow!" said Joey. "That is SO cool!"

Sam's eyes widened and he said, "Thank you, Saja. You've been so nice to us."

Saja turned, smiled at Sam, and gave him a slow, barely-noticeable nod, as his eyes partially closed. He looked at the four friends and motioned them to come closer.

"You are now ready to learn the 3 basic kicks. Should you find yourself in the presence of Napun or his followers, you will need these kicks to survive their attacks. Only a properly-delivered kick to the right area can stop them. Napun and his followers cannot be stopped for good. They can only be temporarily stunned. They are very powerful creatures. If you ever need to use these kicks, it is important that you make them count."

At that moment, Saja placed his right foot behind his left foot. He then drew his arms from his sides, up into fists in front of his chest. He held the left fist a little further away from his body than his right fist. He then tucked his elbows in to his body, lifted his rear heel, and slightly turned his front foot inwards.

"The 3 kicks all begin from this position. It is called the fighting stance. This stance should only be used when danger is present. If you use this stance when there is no danger, it will weaken you. Also, you must never use this stance in anger, nor any of the kicks I am about to teach you. The only time you should use this stance is when you feel fear."

"I understand," said Sally, in a soft, sincere voice.

Billy, Joey and Sam each nodded as they looked at Saja in quiet anticipation.

"Ok, then," continued Saja, "The first kick is the front snap kick. It is best used for short-range attacking. You must pull your toes back so that you strike with the ball of your foot. Like this."

Saja then raised the knee of his rear leg up to his chest. He pointed his ankle downward so that the claws on his feet were pointing towards the ground beneath him. He then pulled the claws on his toes upward while leaving his ankle in the same position. He extended a perfect front snap kick out in front of his chest and held it for several seconds. Joey marveled at Saja's kick as he took mental notes.

"See if you can do this," said Saja to the group.

As the kids attempted to perform the front snap kick, they had difficulty pulling their toes back while keeping their feet flexed at the ankle.

After a few minutes of trying, Billy was able to get the proper position.

"I got it! I got it!" shouted Billy.

"Yes. That is correct," Saja said.

"Ok, I think I've got it, too," said Sally.

"Me too," said Joey.

"I'm still having problems," said Sam, with a slightly sad tone in his voice.

Saja moved closer and touched Sam's foot with his hand. Suddenly, Sam's foot mysteriously moved into the proper position. He now understood what he had been doing wrong. Sam struggled for a moment or two. Then, after trying again, he finally got to where he could create the proper ankle and foot position on the first try.

Saja smiled approvingly and then said, "Next, I will show you the roundhouse kick. It is a deceptive kick, and can be used for getting around obstacles, such as arms or weapons.

Joey, hold your fists up by your face and bring your elbows in to protect your ribs."

Joey's face began to turn a little pale from the thought of Saja kicking him.

The others could hear Joey's throat as he swallowed his saliva. He took a deep breath, nervously blinked several times, and put up his guard to protect against Saja's incoming roundhouse kick.

Joey closed his eyes tightly, as he felt the wind from Saja's kick brush past his face.

Saja had performed a fast, powerful roundhouse kick that stopped half an inch from Joey's eye.

Joey opened his eyes and saw Saja's huge furry foot resting in the air, just off to the side of his face. His eyes opened widely and he nervously looked over at the rest of his friends.

Joey noticed that Saja's foot was kicking with his instep and the lower part of his shin.

"That. Was. Awesome!" exclaimed Joey, at the top of his lungs.

"That would have been painful if it had hit!"

Saja slowly retracted his foot from the side of Joey's face and smiled as he set his powerful leg down on the ground. A small cloud of dust formed around his feet when his claws made contact with the dirt.

"When done with speed and correct technique, this kick can reach a target before your opponent has time to see it coming. The secret is to make sure you begin this kick exactly the same way as the front snap kick. Your opponent should not see the change in direction until it is too late," Saja remarked to Joey.

"I have practiced these kicks for millennia and have developed great control. It is not possible to develop kicks like these unless you spend extra time each day practicing them," continued Saja.

Sally and Sam glanced at each other, as their eyes grew wide as saucers.

"Now, it is your turn," Saja told the kids.

"Get into a fighting stance and place your kicking leg in the back. As you lift your knee, use the same position as the front snap kick. Pivot your supporting foot as much as possible. Allow the toes of the foot you are standing on to point in the opposite direction of your kick. The knee of your kicking leg will become parallel to the ground when you pivot enough. Then, kick in a horizontal fashion, with the top of your foot. Since you are wearing shoes, you will kick with your shoe-laces for the roundhouse kick," said Saja.

The kids tried doing the kick, but could not seem to get their supporting foot to pivot much.

As Saja watched them for a few moments, he said, "It will take extra practice to be able to perform this kick as I have shown you. Be patient, and remember that difficult skills take more time to learn. Working on your flexibility and balance will help you with this kick."

Due to the extra time that Sam needed when he learned the front snap kick, he seemed to have a much better understanding of the roundhouse kick.

As a result, Sam was able to get his foot to pivot before any of the others. There was a look of pride and excitement on his face, as he continued throwing roundhouse kicks in the air.

The others, though, were having difficulty. After several more attempts, Saja could see the look of frustration on their faces. They tried and tried, but could not seem to understand the subtle differences between their kicks, Sam's and Saja's.

Saja then asked the four to sit down on the ground before him.

He paused for a moment to make sure he had their full attention, before speaking. He inhaled, and said, in his soft, raspy voice, "Do you remember the four cornerstones of mental training that I mentioned before you began your first task?"

Billy raised his hand high in the air, until Saja acknowledged him. When Saja's eyes turned to meet Billy's, he spoke up and said, "Wasn't the first one patience?"

Saja smiled and nodded, "Very good, Billy. You remembered. Now, do you remember what I told you about patience?"

"Yes, sir. You said that it would apply the most when I least wanted it to."

"Correct," continued Saja.

"This is one of those times that the word patience applies in your training. I can see that you are all trying very hard. Some things, though, take extra time. Remember that you must be patient with yourselves as you learn. Things come to people at different times and stages of their training. If you see one of your classmates have an easier time learning something, try not to compare yourself with them."

Saja took another deep breath, and, as he exhaled, a faint *hmmmm* came from his throat. He inhaled again, and continued his explanation.............

"You see, Sam struggled a little with learning the front snap kick. But after figuring out what he was not doing, and with a little guidance from me, he eventually got it. Maybe not right away, but he did get it; and because he didn't give up, he probably learned more than anyone else in the group."

Sam smiled, as he lowered his head and looked at the ground. Feeling slightly embarrassed, his cheeks turned a pale red, and he began doodling in the dirt underneath him.

"When you learn something new, there is usually a period of time where none of it makes sense. You may even begin to feel a bit frustrated. It is at these moments that you must learn to take 3 deep breaths. Then, relax, and remember that every master was once a disaster. Although it may be hard to believe, I had great difficulty mastering these kicks, myself.

This is the time for patience," Saja said softly.

"Remember that developing skills takes time. It is much slower in real life than in a video game or a movie. If you continue practicing, you will eventually understand and be able to improve. Once you figure it out, you'll be able to do it with much less effort, as well."

Upon hearing that, the kids stood up, and started practicing again. Sam could see that his friends were still not able to understand how to pivot their supporting foot.

He cleared his throat and, in a soft voice, he said, "Guys, try thinking about spinning in a circle. About half way through the spin, stop. That's when I throw my kick."

You could see a look of understanding wash over the faces of Sam's sister and his two friends. Sam gave a few other thoughts and ideas to them, too. With a little more practice, they all learned how to get their foot to pivot. This allowed them to get the roundhouse kick down well-enough to move on to the third kick.

"You are now ready to learn the final kick," said Saja, as the kid's faces lit up with excitement. The speed of their breathing increased, as they realized they were almost ready to begin the next task.

Saja paused, scanned the trees around them, and said, "The side kick is the most important of all the kicks. If you master this kick, you can learn any other kick. The side kick is a long-range kick that packs a real wallop. It is like the roundhouse kick, in that you pivot your supporting foot. But, you must learn to bring your knee a little further around. For the side kick, bring your knee up towards your chest, so that the bottom of your foot points toward the target.

Only strike with your heel on this kick," Saja continued.

"The most common mistake is not bringing the knee far enough towards the stomach before attempting to kick. Remember, the side kick is called that because you first turn sideways to the target. So, you kick from a sideways position. Then kick with what looks like a 'pushing' action from your hip. Whereas, the roundhouse kick happens more from the knee down; like the front snap kick."

The kids watched in complete amazement, as Saja went to the tree line, grabbed a thick branch, and ripped it from the tree as easily as pulling two pieces of broccoli apart. The sound of the branch being ripped from the tree reminded the kids of a piece of celery slowly being ripped in two.

Saja motioned the kids over, as he removed the leaves, and placed the thick, brown branch against the tree.

"Sally, I want you to break this branch into two pieces," said Saja.

"No problem. I've done this hundreds of times at the park!" Sally replied.

She stepped up to the tree, lifted her knee, and slammed her foot through the thick, brown branch.

The branch shattered into two pieces as Sally's foot continued through the branch, into the tree that it was resting against. Her foot hit and bounced off of the trunk. She lost her balance for a moment and had to catch herself before she fell over.

The sound of the wood snapping startled the creatures that lived in the tree. As they fled the tree top, the fluttering sound of thousands of frantically flapping wings could be heard above before slowly fading off into the distance.

"Very good," Saja said, as he bowed his head towards Sally. "You have just performed a low side kick to break that branch."

A look of understanding came over the faces of the kids. They spread out and started to practice the kick until they were able to perform it as Saja told them.

"You are now ready to begin the next task," Saja told the kids, before turning and heading back towards the forest.

The kids continued practicing the 3 kicks for hours, trying to make them as perfect as possible before beginning the task. One by one, each sat down for what was to be a quick break that turned into a deep slumber, instead.

The kids had had a very long day and dealt with the kind of mental stress that comes with learning to problem-solve.

As they slept, they tossed and turned, dreaming about someday being able to kick like Saja.

Billy snored very loudly, and it attracted the attention of some of the creatures in the area. The creatures came to investigate. When they found the kids sleeping soundly on the ground, they used their noses and nestled some soft material from around the area up under the kids' heads so that they would be more comfortable.

Billy felt the movement around him and slowly opened his eyes, only to see the little creatures quietly giggling, as they scurried back into the forest. He thought it was a cool dream, closed his eyes again, and went back to snoring.

When morning finally came, the kids woke. They had fallen asleep right next to the character that Saja had etched on the ground for their protection.

They yawned and stretched. They then went down to the babbling brook to wash the dirt off their faces and drank a bit more of the magical water.

After eating a light breakfast of some of the local fruits growing on the trees, they decided it was time to tackle the second task.

Sally instructed the group as they got into their fighting positions.

On Sally's command, the four friends raised their knees high, and executed fast, powerful front snap kicks at head level. They were all able to hold their kicks for a full two seconds before bringing their knees back to a bent position.

They were extra careful not to allow their legs to fall to the ground. Instead, they rechambered their kicks so that it looked like they could throw another one without setting their feet down.

They did the same thing with the roundhouse and then the side kick. As they completed their side kicks and held the kicks in the air for the full two seconds, they heard the first bell ring.

They formed a circle and giggled, as they jumped up and down while holding on to each other's shoulders.

They then sat down to discuss what they had learned.

After several minutes, it became clear to them that they had to use patience and persistence to complete this task.

Sam also added that he seemed to learn more when he taught the technique to others than by just working on his kicks alone. This was because he had to take the time to think about how to explain it. And that made him have to think more about it, himself.

At the end of Sam's statement, they heard the second bell.

Sally reached into her pocket and removed the scroll again. As she began unrolling it, the ground beneath them began to shake and tremble.

Chapter
Six

The kids looked in every direction, but could not pinpoint what was causing the ground to tremble.

They figured it must be an earth quake!

Sally shoved the scroll back into her pocket before they had time to look at it.

She began looking for a safe place to hide, and sprinted towards a very tall tree as the others followed closely behind her. Without any hesitation, they each leapt onto the tree. The sound of the rubber from their shoes grinded into the rough, thick bark. They hurriedly climbed until they were about half way up the tree, past the first several branches, and out of sight.

As they stopped climbing, the ground began to shake more fiercely.

Then, the sound of big, heavy hooves became clear to the kids.

A huge cloud of dust formed over the horizon, and they could hear voices. The voices sounded like what they imagined a group of angry green ogre's voices would sound like.

They couldn't make out what was being said, but they could hear that it sounded serious.

Within about 20 or 30 seconds, the creatures passed by the tree. Their leader was another lion man! He was wearing a rusty, bronze breast plate, and other types of strange armor. He let out an angry roar that quieted all the insects and creatures in the area.

"They must be around here somewhere. I can smell them," said the lion man.

Napun's minions were massive creatures that did, in fact, look something like what the kids imagined ogres would look like. Their arms and legs were like huge tree trunks, with hardened brown claws for finger and toe nails. They had large patches of blue fur on their bodies. Their skin was scaly, and they had very large foreheads. They had beady little eyes that were sunk back into their skulls a few inches.

They paused with Napun and sniffed strongly in an attempt to catch the scent of the four friends. Fortunately, though, the sweet smell from the large flowers on the tree that they were hiding in masked their scent.

"I-I-It's him........that must be Napun," whispered Sally to the others.

"What should we do?" asked Sam.

"I need a minute to think," replied Sally.

The kids sat quietly in the tree, as Napun and his minions searched the area. They searched this way and that, looking for the four friends, (whom they now viewed as enemies after observing Saja teaching them).

Fortunately for the kids, Saja had created another etching not far from them, and the essence from it began to make Napun and his minions feel weak.

"Quick, back the way we came from. Saja has been here, and one of his etchings is close by."

As Napun moved through the crowd of his minions, they turned and began following him, the ground trembling with every step of their huge feet. The minions left imprints on the ground that were over an inch deep.

When they were out of sight, the rumbling and shaking faded off into the distance, and the kids climbed back down the tree.

"Whew! That was a close one!" yelled Joey to the group.

"Yes. I'm not sure what I would have done if they had spotted us," Billy added.

"Well, we can't worry about that right now. We've got two more tasks we have to complete, and we don't have much time," said Sally, as she cautiously glanced at her watch.

As Sally reached in and took out the scroll again, she noticed the second green checkmark had appeared, and then the third task was revealed:

Scroll of Mingyun
Task Three

You have successfully completed two tasks now. The third task is to master the three basic blocks, and one important strike: the low block, middle block, upper block, and the reverse punch. Your skills will be tested by the elements.

The kids read the scroll a second time and then the three boys, with very puzzled looks on their faces, looked towards Sally. Scratching his chin, Sam asked, "The elements? What's THAT supposed to mean?"

Sally searched for an answer, but could not come up with anything that sounded good.

She let out a long sigh as she slowly shook her head from side to side. "I honestly don't know, either."

Joey, with a tone of frustration in his voice, added, "Well, how are we going to know when we complete this task then?!"

They sat in silence for a few minutes, feeling defeated, as the now-familiar humming sound could be heard nearby. The kids smiled and jumped to their feet. They knew what it meant.

They figured they would be able to get the answers they needed from Saja.

As they approached, Saja was finishing up another etching of protection. He saw the kids coming and motioned them over.

He spent the next several minutes teaching them the techniques listed on the scroll.

While the kids worked on them, Saja observed and offered insights to make their blocks better.

"Each block must have a twisting action in the wrist. Without the twist you will not be able to complete this task," he told the kids.

Before you begin to block, your fist must be turned in the opposite direction of its ending position. Otherwise, you will not have enough power to defend against the elements."

Sam looked over at Saja and spoke up, "Elements? What are these 'elements', Saja?"

There was an extended moment of silence as the kids waited for his reply. Saja's face became somber.

"Unfortunately, Sam, I am not permitted to answer this question.

It is forbidden.

Part of this task is observation. I'm afraid you must discover the answer for yourselves."

Saja noticed the disappointment in the kids' body language as they contemplated the meaning of what he had just told them.

"This will be your most challenging task, yet," Saja said to the kids. He then stroked his long, gray beard as it glistened in the sunlight.

"It is time for you to master the reverse punch," said Saja, moving closer to a very large tree nearby.

"This tree has been standing for 850 years. I planted this one, myself. Come and look at it."

There was a large section of the trunk that was smooth and had no bark. It had been indented with huge marks of what looked like knuckle prints all over it.

"I have used this tree to practice the reverse punch for many years, and now, you must use it for the same purpose.

I will demonstrate once for you, and then it will be your turn to try. You must each punch the tree 10 times, until you are able to leave your knuckle marks on it," Saja told them. He then prepared to demonstrate the punch for the kids.

He closed his blue eyes, took a long, deep breath, and drew his elbow back behind him. He made sure that his fist rested against his rib cage.

Saja slowly opened his eyes and silently stared at the tree for a few seconds while he took several slow, deep breaths.

Then, without warning, he quickly struck the tree with a reverse punch, and let out an ear-piercing yell upon impact.

The entire tree shook, and hundreds of leaves suddenly fell from the branches and floated to the ground.

Saja's fist made a huge imprint on the tree, leaving indentations where his knuckles made contact with it.

The kids stood in silence, stunned at what they had just seen.

"Unbelievable!" said Sally.

"How did you do that?!" asked Joey.

Sam and Billy looked at the tree with their mouths wide open and their arms hanging lifelessly at their sides.

The sound of the punch, and the crackling of the wood, as Saja's knuckles penetrated and smashed into the old tree, scared every living creature in the area.

The kids knew that they would have to try next. They became apprehensive at the very thought of striking a tree with their bare hands!

Saja allowed a few moments to pass, and then broke the silence, "Sam, it is your turn. Step up to the tree."

Sam slowly closed his mouth, turned his head to the left and looked at Billy for a brief moment. With an obvious look of doubt on his face, he moved into position in front of the tree.

"Make a strong front stance. Pull your fist near your ribs, and be sure that your fist is turned upside down, high on your ribs. When you are ready, turn your fist over at the very last moment. Strike the tree with the first two knuckles with all your might. When the punch lands, your palm must be facing the ground, as if you were going to drop something."

Sam did as instructed, and just as he looked like he was going to throw the punch, he stopped, and said, "I can't. I'm afraid, Saja." His voice was quivering uncontrollably and he did his best to avoid making eye contact with Saja.

"Relax, Sam. You can do it," Saja told him. "Concentrate.

Use the three rules of focus.

Focus your eyes. Look at the target. Stare at it.

Focus your mind. Picture the target in your mind. Imagine your fist striking perfectly and leaving your knuckle imprints right under mine.

Focus your body. Get into position and feel the power coming from your feet. Allow the power to come up through your legs, up through your waist and into your fist as you execute the technique.

If you do not allow fear to control you, you will be fine, Sam."

Sam calmed himself and got back into position. He thought through the 3 rules of focus one last time. He then gave a loud thundering yell; a yell so loud that even his own ears hurt.

He then threw his strongest punch at the tree, striking with only his first two knuckles, as Saja had instructed.

As the loud, dull thud from Sam's fist struck the tree, everyone gasped in surprise. When Sam pulled back his fist, they saw the imprints from his knuckles on the tree trunk, right under Saja's!

"I want to go next!" said Joey.

Joey stepped up to the tree and thought about the advice that Saja had given Sam. Joey hit the tree with all his force and also left *his* knuckle imprints on the trunk.

Then, Sally, and finally, Billy.

There were now four new sets of small knuckle prints on the tree under Saja's.

Saja smiled at them, and then a look of seriousness came over his weathered face, before he spoke again.

"You have mastered the 3 blocks and the reverse punch in record time; much faster than any of my other pupils, in fact.

You have done well. But, you must now head in that direction to complete this task."

Saja pointed off into the distance, past a large row of oddly-shaped blue and green hedges that lined an open meadow.

"Unfortunately, the Meadow of Gan Nan is the one place in our world that I am not permitted to place my etchings of protection. You must make it to the other side of the meadow, where I have already completed an etching for you."

The tone of his voice worried Sally. She knew there was something Saja wanted to tell them, but he could not.

The kids thanked Saja and started on their journey.

As they hopped over the hedges and headed out into the vast quiet, open meadow, they were talking about all they had learned so far.

All of a sudden, a strong wind began to blow around them. It grew stronger and stronger. This wind was different than any other wind they had experienced before. It blew even more strongly as it took the shape of four large gray hammers, directly in front of each of the kids.

"Spread out!" yelled Sally, over the sound of the fierce wind.

"Do it. Now!"

The boys moved away from each other, as the wind-hammers followed each of them.

Suddenly, the hammers darted up, high into the sky above them.

The first one came down with the force of a heat-seaking missile at Sally.

In the back of her mind, she heard Saja's words about twisting her blocks.

She quickly placed her right arm across her left hip with her palm facing upward.

As the large gray wind-hammer approached, Sally exhaled and executed a perfect upper block. It struck the handle of the hammer and sent it rushing back into the air.

The hammer came down at her again, and she blocked again with the other arm!

Her second block shattered the wind-hammer into two pieces! Then, it suddenly vanished into a puff of eerie, thick, gray smoke; just as quickly as it had appeared.

The boys had very similar experiences. They were able to successfully block and destroy their wind-hammers, too.

"RUN!" yelled Sally.

The four friends then took off in full-sprint mode. They ran towards the edge of the meadow, hoping to reach it before anything else happened.

The Meadow of Gan Nan was very, very vast. It was miles across. Although, from the other side of the hedges, it looked much smaller to the kids.

As they continued running, it began to pour rain. It rained like the kids had never experienced before.

The ground beneath their feet began to get wet and soggy, which made the ground muddy. The mud sucked their feet into itself. Each step made a loud sloshing noise that sounded like something most kids might find amusing.

But, this was no time to laugh. The slimy, brown mud made it very difficult for the kids to move.

Their legs began to get tired, and their lungs were now burning from breathing so fast and hard.

As the kids stopped and bent over to catch their breath, the pounding rain suddenly transformed into large translucent, four-foot cylinders in front of each of them.

The rain-cylinders began violently slashing at them in a left-to-right motion and it greatly frightened the kids. Droplets of water from the cylinders whipped them in the faces as they managed to avoid direct contact with them.

The kids knew what was about to happen.

Without a word, they made a small circle and turned their backs to each other. The rain-cylinders followed their movements and lined up with each of the kids.

Billy's cylinder attacked first. It moved up towards Billy's face. The splashes of water made it hard for him to see.

Billy trusted his instincts and knew that this time he wouldn't be able to rely on using his eyes. Instead, he closed them and listened intently to determine where the cylinder was.

He waited for it to make a sound as it suddenly slashed at his left thigh.

Without another thought, Billy brought his left fist up near his right ear. He drove his arm downward at a forty-five degree angle, and blocked the rain-cylinder.

Unfortunately, Billy forgot to twist his fist at the very end of his block, and the rain-cylinder struck him on his left arm.

The block hurt Billy.

He let out a pained groan, as he grimaced.

"Ow!" screamed Billy.

The rain-cylinder then quickly rose up again, and came down at his other thigh.

This time, Billy remembered to twist his fist. When he made contact with the cylinder, it fell to the wet ground and melted into the dark muck beneath his feet.

Billy yelled out to his friends, "Remember to twist your block! Don't forget to twist your block!"

The other rain-cylinders swiped at the legs of Sally, Sam, and Joey.

Using the skills they had developed during the third task, they successfully destroyed the cylinders.

They high-fived each other and began trudging forward again through the mud.

The mud seemed to get stickier with each step, which slowed them down even more.

Each lift of their legs took more and more energy out of their small bodies, and they grew weary.

They were just about to reach the end of the meadow. They were still trudging through mud, when the gooey mud began to form up in front of them!

The mud transformed into one large, brown, gloppy fist.

With no warning, it swung at Sally.

She quickly ducked under it just in time.

Then, it turned and swung at Sam next.

Sam jumped over it and landed on the other side of it with a look of complete shock on his face.

The huge mud-fist turned and swung at Joey's ear.

Joey remembered the middle block. Without another moment to prepare, he executed a very powerful middle block that caught the mud-fist just below its base.

Mud flew everywhere!

Some of it even got into Joey's eyes, which prevented him from being able to see properly.

Sally ran to Joey and wiped the mud from his eyes with the sleeve of her jacket.

Just then, the huge mud-fist set its sights on Billy.

It sped up significantly, and took three quick swings at him.

Billy backed up and made the first two swings miss completely. Then, he folded his arms across his chest, and took a deep breath. He turned the palm of his fist downward, and blocked as quickly and strongly as he could possibly block. And, he made sure to twist his fist at the very end of the block.

He also yelled strongly to add more power and speed to his block.

Upon impact, the massive mud-fist shattered into a thousand pieces and dropped to the ground.

The rain suddenly stopped, and the ground dried almost instantly.

The four friends then made a mad dash for the edge of the Meadow of Gan Nan.

As they approached the edge, they could see Saja's etching of protection up ahead.

THUNK!

Sally bounced heavily off of something very solid.

BANG!

Billy, too.

Sam then ran into Billy's back. Joey almost trampled over Sam as they came to a screeching halt, without any idea of what hit them.

It was a powerful force field. They could see a glowing, silver lever on the other side of the force field. The kids had seen enough sci-fi television to know what it was.

"Guys, we can't get through here. There's a force field blocking us," Sally said.

They spread out and each of them care-fully touched the force field. They each tried feeling for an opening along the perimeter of the meadow.

They could not find one, no matter how far they moved in either direction.

"Wait," said Sally. "We had to use our 3 blocks to defeat the elements."

The kids looked at each other, nodded their heads, and said, in unison, "The elements! Now we know what they were! The wind, the rain, and the mud!!"

"Yes," Sally continued, "So we have one last technique that we haven't used yet; the reverse punch.

Maybe if we all strike the force field at the same time, we can cause it to short-circuit."

The four friends each spread out about 20 feet from each other. They took their strongest front stances, and waited for Sally to count it down.

"THREE.........TWO...............ONE.... GO!"

The sound of the four punches happening all at once was deafening. *KA-BAM!* The entire meadow grew completely silent.

Nothing happened.

They drew their fists back a second time. *KA-BAM!*

Still nothing.

Then, Sam remembered the 5 tenets on the three smaller scrolls that Saja had given them. *Perseverance* and *Indomitable Spirit* immediately popped into his mind.

"Keep going!" yelled Sam.

As the friends gritted their teeth, they continued pounding their fists against the seemingly indestructible force field.

One. Then two. Then three. Then four punches.

Just when the kids began to really doubt themselves, Sally shouted, "One more time! We've got this!!"

With that, the four friends mustered up one last brave attempt.

They closed their eyes and visualized the outcome. They inhaled, and, in what seemed like slow-motion, released their most powerful punches so far. Sweat flew from their fists, as Joey gritted his teeth and snarled like a caged tiger.

The impact was incredible. *BOOOOOOOOOOOOOOM!*

When their fists connected with the force field, it flickered and blinked two times. Then, it suddenly vanished.

The kids collapsed to the ground into a pile of leaves that had blown onto the etching of protection when the force field disintegrated.

They could hardly hear the sound of the first bell over their own heavy breathing, as they tried to recover their energy.

They discussed all that they had been through. The four friends felt that persistence and bravery were the most important lessons learned from this task.

The second bell rang, as the kids fell asleep on the etching, unable to stay awake any longer.

Chapter
Seven

Sally awoke nearly an hour later. The others were sound asleep, Billy snoring again, like a hairy, wild hog with a bad cold.

"Wake up guys. Wake up. Wake up," Sally repeated.

The boys slowly opened their eyes and Joey let out a long, loud, growling yawn and wiped his eyes.

"What? What's going on? Why do we have to wake up?" asked Billy through another long yawn before closing his eyes again.

"Don't you want to see what the final task is?" asked Sally.

Billy's eyes opened and his mouth closed, "The final task?" as he suddenly remembered where he was and why he was there.

"Oh...... the final task. Yes! Open the scroll!"

Sally already had the scroll in her hand. Once it was unrolled, she noticed the pretty green checkmark next to the third task. Then, the final task began to appear.

Scroll of Mingyun
Final Task

The final task is to overcome your fear and defeat the evil Napun to restore balance to this universe. If you are successful at this task, you will hear only one bell. When the bell rings you will have six hours to return to the original etching of protection. There you will be transported back to your world. If you do not make it in time, you will remain here permanently.

Upon reading the final task, the kids sat in silence, stunned by the words they had read. A look of doubt crept over each of the four friends' faces.

Several moments passed, and then a sound startled them.

From behind one of the nearby bushes, they could see something moving.

The kids crouched down together and slowly snuck towards the bush. Sam began pulling at Joey's pant legs.

"Let's go back. I'm afraid it's Napun," whispered Sam.

Joey turned his head around, and placed his index finger over his lips. "Shhhhh. Be quiet, or he'll hear us."

The kids continued inching closer towards the bush. They got about two feet from it, when one of Napun's minions sprung up from behind the bush. He snarled and glared at the kids, and called out to the other minions!

Before he could say too much, Sally hopped onto his back. She reached around his massive head and covered his enormous mouth with both hands.

"Hurry up! Help me!" Sally cried out.

"Sam, grab his legs!

Billy, grab his arms!

Joey, grab him around the waist and don't let go!"

The boys each did as instructed. Working together, they pulled the minion to the ground. Sally used her feet and latched onto some nearby vines. She wriggled and pulled until she was able to grab them.

"Joey, take this vine and tie it around his waist. Quickly! Before he can get up!" she yelled.

Joey was able to get it around the minion's waist. Then, he pulled the vine up around the minion's neck and was able to tie his wrists together.

Sally then tossed the other vine to Sam. Sam tied the vine around the minion's feet very tightly.

Once they were sure he couldn't use his arms, Billy let go. The kids then stood over the minion, watching frightfully, as he struggled to free himself.

"Stop struggling," Sally told him.

"And be quiet! Or else!"

The minion ignored her, and continued wriggling and writhing on the ground in a complete fit.

His grunts and groans were very frightening, and the kids worried that he might break free.

They backed up and prayed that the vines would hold.

They knew, though, that it wouldn't be long before he would get loose and attack them.

The minion let out a blood-curdling primal scream......a scream that pierced the kid's ears.

In stark fear, the kids fell backwards onto the ground.

They frantically tried to back up! Kicking into the hard, dusty ground beneath them, they tried to push away from the evil minion.

After several fluttering kicks to the ground to propel themselves backward and create some space, the kids stumbled to their feet.

Their hearts pounded as fear gripped each of them. They began running in the opposite direction of the minion while their hearts beat through their shirts.

The minion then snapped the vines from around his arms and legs. He growled, stood up, and motioned to his 3 friends, who had heard his scream and were now coming to his rescue.

Napun was also with them. He was carrying a large stick, and when he saw the kids, he bolted forward in their direction.

The four friends saw Napun and nearly fainted. They wished that Saja was here to save them from this unexpected situation.

"Hurry! He's going to catch us!" cried Sally.

Napun and the four minions were beginning to catch up to the kids.

Unsure of what else to do, they ran as quickly as they had ever ran in their entire lives.

Suddenly, Joey remembered that Saja said he would be nearby and to call out if they ever needed him.

"Saja! Saja! Help!

We need you!

Please! Help!" yelled Sam at the top of his lungs.

The kids could feel Napun's hot breath on the backs of their necks as he closed in on them.

As he reached out to grab Billy by the shirt, a lightning bolt crashed through the air, and struck Napun in the chest.

He was propelled backwards by the force of the lightning bolt....only it wasn't a lightning bolt at all. It was a powerful flying side kick, thrown by Saja.

Saja had heard Joey's cry, and he leapt into the air and kicked Napun before he could grab Billy. Napun's rusty bronze breastplate shattered into 3 pieces.

He fell to the ground, as his minions gasped in disbelief.

"Leave this place now," Saja said in a very strict tone. His normally-friendly eyes now had a look of serious intent in them.

Napun stood, and rubbed his chest where Saja had struck him.

"I have been waiting for this day for a very long time," Napun said. "Now, I will destroy you."

Saja stood calmly with his arms tucked into the sleeves of his dark robe. The sunlight cast a shadow over half of Saja's face as his piercing blue eyes stared intently at Napun.

He spoke in a tone that the kids had not heard before, "That would be a mistake, Napun."

Napun tilted his head backwards towards the sky and laughed heartily. He then snarled and let out a huge roar that echoed through the forest trees.

Creatures scattered in every direction. All the kids could hear was the sound of their own hearts beating.

Napun jumped into the air, spun twice, and landed a kick against the left side of Saja's face.

The kids ran to Saja to help him, but as they neared him, Napun's minions intercepted them.

The four minions surrounded the kids. With fangs exposed and dripping with saliva, the minions glared at the kids. They then began growling like wild beasts.

The fact was they *were* wild beasts, and they towered over the kids.

With no other alternative but to protect themselves, the kids spread out from each other. Sally, Joey, Sam and Billy now each had their own opponent.

Billy's minion attacked first. He rushed towards Billy. Each footstep made the ground shake beneath him.

Billy waited until the creature was right in front of him before acting. As the minion attempted to kick Billy in the left thigh with his huge, scaly, tree-trunk of a leg, Billy stepped back into a strong back stance. He then executed a very powerful low block to the minion's leg.

As Billy's forearm struck the minion directly on the shin, the creature let out a loud, pained howl.

He began hopping around on one foot, the ground quaking with each hop.

The minion regained his composure and charged again.

He raged forward to club Billy over the head with a hammer fist strike. Billy threw a powerful side kick that landed directly into the minion's stomach and lifted him into the air and knocked him back at least four feet. He landed on his back with a huge thud. Dust and dirt flew from the ground, and the minion was out cold.

Upon seeing this, Sally's minion attacked.

The creature charged like a huge, angry bull towards Sally and head-butted her in the stomach.

Sally exhaled strongly as she went flying backwards into a tree that stopped her fall.

She used the tree as a barrier between herself and the minion.

He charged at her again. He slashed at Sally as she moved behind the tree. His large claws grazed the tree and took several inches of wood out of it. The wind from the powerful strike made Sally's long auburn hair fly in all directions.

Always known for thinking quickly, she ran and slid under the minion's feet and popped up behind him.

She then delivered a powerful side kick to his back. The kick knocked him forward, forcing him to hit his head on the tree with a massive thud. The curvy lines of the tree bark were now visible on the minion's forehead.

Slightly dazed, he turned towards Sally, snarled and beat his chest with both fists several times.

He yelled as he charged in again, "*RRRRAAAAAAAAAA*!!"

The minion threw a very powerful punch to Sally's face. She moved slightly to the right, ending up in a horse stance, and blocked the beast's punch with her very best middle block.

Like a boom of thunder, she struck the minion directly in the solar plexus with a reverse punch, that sent him to the ground.

As he fell, his head bounced off of the ground and he was out cold. His huge, hairy tongue was now hanging out of his mouth, and his breathing began to sound like short, quick snorts.

Meanwhile, Saja was still dealing with Napun.

Napun had become enraged, as he noticed two of his minions, defeated by the kids, laying on the ground nearby.

He looked at the minions, snapped his head in Sally's direction and glared at her as he huffed.

At that very moment, Saja took advantage of Napun's distraction. He struck him in the thigh with a powerful roundhouse kick that made Napun fall to his knee.

Saja stepped back and waited for Napun to make the next move.

Napun did not disappoint.

He picked up the stick he was carrying, and used it to stand back up to his feet. He brushed off his knee, and began swinging the staff in a whirlwind of fury, as he roared again.

Without another moment's notice, Joey's minion struck.

He jumped high into the air. On the way down, he struck at Joey's head in a clubbing action. The minion meant to pound him into the ground like a sledge hammer hitting a rail road spike.

Joey remembered the lessons that Saja had taught him, and the tasks that he had already completed.

It all led to this very moment.

Time seemed to slow down for Joey, as he prepared his response. He took his left fist across his body. His right elbow was tucked in to his ribs; his right fist pointing directly at the minion, who was now striking at Joey's head.

Joey remembered to twist his fist, as he blocked the minion's powerful strike, using an upper block.

The power of the block completely stopped the minion's strike, causing it to be deflected off to the side of Joey's body.

The minion lost his balance and fell forward. Joey shifted into a strong front stance and executed a reverse punch that landed squarely on the minion's jaw and knocked him out cold.

Patches of blue fur, and a fang, flew from the minion's now-expressionless face.

The minion fell to the ground with a huge *THUD*.

The last of the minions then attacked Sam. Sam was still unsure of himself. He backed up as far as he could before having to deal with his minion.

The minion swung his huge leg at Sam's. Instinctively, Sam jumped up over it. The wind from the kick nearly knocked him over.

Sam suddenly remembered the third of the smaller scrolls. The one that read *Respect, Focus and Discipline are your allies on any quest.*

At that moment, he focused his mind on what was happening to him.

He stared intently into the eyes of the minion, while thinking only one thought...... survival.

He focused his body by assuming his very best fighting stance. He held his fists in front of him, elbows tucked in, weight forward, back heel raised.

As the minion launched his next attack, Sam performed a solid front snap kick to the knee of the minion.

"*OOOOOF*," gasped the minion.

As he bent over in great pain, Sam unleashed 4 quick punches to the midsection of the minion, knocking him to the ground.

Sally, Joey and Billy then surrounded the huge, fallen creature.

They gazed at him with a sense of confidence that can only come from successfully completing tasks like the Tam Gu. The kids now realized that they were much stronger than they gave themselves credit for.

The angry look in the minion's eyes suddenly changed.

He could see that he was outnumbered. He got to his feet, turned around, and ran towards the forest, disappearing into the trees and leaving Napun to fend for himself.

Just then, the kids heard a loud *"CRACK!"*

It was Saja.

Napun had swung his staff at Saja, and Saja used a block that the kids had not seen before.

The block shattered the staff into two pieces. Saja then unleashed a series of kicks upon Napun.

He kicked with his left leg, then his right. Then, without putting his foot down, he kicked 4 more times to Napun's midsection and face, and sent him hurtling backwards.

Napun caught himself by digging his heels in to the ground to stop his body's uncontrollable backwards motion. Dirt and dust flew up from his feet as the ground finally brought him to a complete halt.

He grunted, roared, and charged again.

Saja spun quickly and threw a spinning wheel kick that landed on the right side of Napun's face.

Napun saw stars.

Without stopping the motion of his spinning wheel kick, Saja dropped to the ground and executed a second kick. His lightning-fast low spinning wheel kick caught Napun at the ankle and knocked him off his feet.

As if in a dream, time slowed down, while Napun floated helplessly in the air for what seemed like several extended seconds.

Then he came down hard.

WHAM!

Napun hit the ground and the fight was over.

Saja nonchalantly placed his hands back inside the sleeves of his robe, and politely bowed to the now-fallen Napun.

Napun slowly picked himself up and realized that he had made a huge mistake by ever betraying Saja. He threw himself down at the feet of Saja, and begged for forgiveness.

There was a long pause from Saja. He contemplated how he was going to respond to this unexpected gesture of remorse from Napun, his former student.

In a bit of surprise to the kids, Saja reached out, touched Napun on the left shoulder, and gave him a gentle squeeze with his enormous paw.

"Napun, I forgive you.

I never wanted it to come to this.

I was once young like you, and I made my share of mistakes, too.

As long as you have learned from your mistakes, I cannot hold a grudge against you.

Part of mastering life is making mistakes.

Without making mistakes, one cannot gain wisdom or enlightenment.

There is an old saying that good judgment comes from experience, and a lot of experience happens as a result of bad judgment."

Napun began sobbing, as he lowered his head, and realized that Saja was right.

"Thank you, Saja.

I now understand that I made a mistake when I taught these creatures the fighting techniques you taught me.

These creatures are easily angered and are full of hatred.

Teaching them your fighting skills only made them more dangerous.

I will make sure to teach them the traits of patience, respect, modesty, and honesty."

Saja's eyes slowly returned to the peaceful look that the four friends were used to, and he nodded at Napun.

Napun stood, bowed politely and shook Saja's one hand with both of his own.

He then turned, and helped his fallen minions to their feet. With one last look at Saja and the four friends, Napun and his minions headed back into the forest and disappeared from sight.

Saja turned to the kids and asked them if they were alright.

The kids, standing in complete silence and awe; eyes opened widely, nodded slowly at Saja.

"You have completed the quest," said Saja, approaching Sam with a look of pride in his eyes.

Sam, head held high, reached out to Saja to shake his hand. As Saja's massive hand made contact with Sam's, he pulled him in close and hugged him.

"I'm very proud of you, Sam, for finding your inner lion, and displaying such courage throughout this quest."

Sam felt the love in Saja's words, as he closed his eyes and embraced him for several seconds.

The others gathered in and hugged Saja, as well.

Saja then backed up a step, so he could look them in the eyes.

"You have helped us to restore balance to our universe. I couldn't be prouder of each of you.

You have already learned a great deal in your short time here. There is much I have left to teach you, but now it is time for you to return home."

Just then, the final bell rang from the silver box.

The kids bowed to Saja and said their goodbyes. He pointed the way for them to return to the original etching of protection.

They began their journey back, as each recounted their own personal battles with the minions. There was an extra level of excitement in their stride, as they continued back to the etching.

Time was ticking, though, and they had a long way to travel still.

The kids stopped to catch their breath, and grab a quick drink of the magical water before continuing on. They leaned against a big rock and closed their eyes for a moment to rest.

Without realizing it, the kids fell asleep and four hours quickly passed.

Sally was jolted awake by the dream she was having, and she woke the others up. They then hurried on their way.

"Wow," said Sally. "I still can't believe all this actually happened. It seems so unbelievable," she continued.

"Yes. No one would believe us if we were to try and tell them, would they?" laughed Joey.

"No, I suppose not," Billy agreed.

Sam just shrugged his shoulders and kept walking.

As they approached the original etching of protection, they could see that it was glowing brightly. The light looked exactly like the light from the silver box, and it began pulsing very quickly.

Sally looked down at her watch, and realized that a lot more time had transpired than she had originally thought.

Time was running out for the kids!

"Hurry!" yelled Sally.

"We only have minutes before we get stuck here for good!"

The boys picked up their speed. As they neared, Sam ran several steps, leapt into the air and landed directly onto the middle of the glowing etching of protection.

Sally, Joey, and Billy also stepped onto it, and then suddenly the pulsing white light changed to one large, continuous white beam of light.

The kids closed their eyes and hoped for the best.

In an instant, they were transported back to the park, at the exact moment before they found the box.

The weather was exactly the same. Sally looked down at her watch again, and it said 8:45am, just about the time it was before they got zapped into Saja's universe.

They looked around, and realized that it was as if they had never left in the first place.

The kids took turns staring at each other and back at the park, not sure what to say about it.

Just then, they heard the sounds of the other neighborhood kids arriving for today's baseball game.

Sally felt her pocket for the silver box and the scroll, but they were gone now.

The four friends smiled at each other, and ran to meet the others. They were very happy to be home again.

They remembered that completing the quest was supposed to grant them with special powers that would make them more successful in everything that they did.

Teams were chosen, and the game began. Nobody knew what Sally, Sam, Joey and Billy had just gone through.

During the game, the four friends played their very best baseball game EVER.

The other kids looked on with awe.

"Sam, when did you learn to run so fast?" asked one of the neighborhood kids.

"You were always fast, but never THAT fast!"

Sam, shrugged and said, "I don't know. I've just been practicing some new exercises that must have made my legs stronger."

Billy was also much better during the game. He was the team's pitcher; already known for throwing the fastest fast-balls of any other kid in the neighborhood. But today, he was able to throw faster than ever before. Billy was able to strike out almost every player on the other team.

Joey, happy to be holding onto his favorite bat again, hit five home runs during the game. Three of which, flew over the fence, past the parking lot and into the Feldman's back yard. The Feldman's dog quickly tore the baseballs into shreds with his teeth, as his tail wagged a million miles per hour.

His large, silver, water-stained dish flew in the air and fell to the ground with a loud, metallic thud, when one of the balls landed right in his food and scattered it everywhere.

Sally also played her very best game. She was able to steal all the bases twice and was also able to tag a runner before he made it to first base. Then, to everyone's amazement, she ran all the way from first base and caught an intended-bunt that ended up being the final out in the 9th inning.

The kids were victorious. The other neighborhood kids were in complete amazement. They were simply stunned by the mysteriously-improved skills of the four friends on that baseball diamond that day.

Without realizing it, completing the Tam Gu helped the four friends in ways they couldn't begin to imagine.

After the game, the kids went their separate ways, excited about going home to see their parents again.

When they arrived home, they hugged their parents tightly and told them how much they loved them.

The parents were a little surprised by this, because the only time their kids behaved this way was when it was either their birthday or Christmas!

Whatever the reason, though, the parents appreciated their kids' behavior and hoped it didn't change back any time soon.

"So," said Sally and Sam's mom, "What did you do today? Did you have a good day?"

Sally and Sam tried to hide their grins, as their eyes met each other's.

"Mom, you wouldn't believe me if I told you, but we had a VERY good day today!"

"Oh, honey. That's such great news," said their mother.

"I'm just glad you had a good time. I have dinner ready in the kitchen. Why don't you and Sammy come, sit down, and tell me all about it?"

Sally, Sam and their parents had a lovely conversation before asking if they could head off to bed.

As the kids went upstairs, mom and dad stood at the bottom of the stairs, hugging each other lovingly.

"Good night kids," said their father.

"Good night, dad," replied the kids, as they rounded the corner and headed for their bedrooms.

"Old Saja. I had no idea that our kids would get to meet him, too," said Sam and Sally's dad.

"It seems like just yesterday when YOU found that little silver box all those years ago."

"I know honey," she replied. "I wonder if we should tell them about OUR quest. I don't know if they'd even believe us."

"Probably not," said dad, as he squeezed her hand and kissed her cheek. He then turned and walked towards the living room to sit down for his evening reading. "Probably not."

About the Author

James Theros was born in Indianapolis, Indiana in February of 1969. He is the oldest of 3 siblings and has 4 kids of his own. He got started in martial arts at the age of 7 at an after school program and fell in love with the training and immediately knew that it would become his career. He opened Level 10 Martial Arts College in the summer of 1995 in Indianapolis, Indiana. He and his wife, Debi moved to Florida in 2017 with their award winning martial arts program. James has worked with thousands of students from ages 3 through 85, teaching them martial arts, leadership, and success principles.

His students say that the training he offers has changed their lives for the better and he frequently has former students reach out to thank him for the impact his program has had on them.

James and Debi Theros are favorites with school teachers and principals, alike, because of the work that they've done in the local school systems to help bring more respect, focus and discipline into the school's classrooms. They are frequently invited to speak to students and faculty members on a variety of topics.

James enjoys story-telling and creative writing. He also hosts a weekly podcast that can be found on iTunes, and writes regularly for magazines.

For more information about the author, visit him on Facebook, YouTube, or his school websites:

www.palmharborkarate.com
www.level10martialarts.com
www.ltkfa.com

James is available for speaking engagements or seminars and can be reached through Facebook, Linkedin.com, or any of the websites mentioned above.

CPSIA information can be obtained
at www.ICGtesting.com
Printed in the USA
FFOW03n1220090318
45515167-46255FF

9 780990 416418